HEADSPARKS

HEADSPARKS

by ROBERT COLES

An Atlantic Monthly Press Book

Little, Brown and Company

Boston   Toronto

FIRST EDITION

T 04/75

Library of Congress Cataloging in Publication Data

Coles, Robert.
  Headsparks.

  "An Atlantic Monthly Press book."
  SUMMARY: A sixteen-year-old girl finds the
pressures of adolescence an increasingly unbearable
mental strain.
  I. Title.
PZ7.C6777He   [Fic]   74-32046
ISBN 0-316-15156-4

ATLANTIC–LITTLE, BROWN BOOKS
ARE PUBLISHED BY
LITTLE, BROWN AND COMPANY
IN ASSOCIATION WITH
THE ATLANTIC MONTHLY PRESS

Published simultaneously in Canada
by Little, Brown & Company (Canada) Limited

PRINTED IN THE UNITED STATES OF AMERICA

Again, to Jane and to our sons:

Bob, Dan and Mike

HEADSPARKS

Nothing like this had happened before. Cathy was standing in Simpson's drugstore and she had no idea why she had come or for how long she had been there. The druggist was staring at her.

"Is anything the matter?"

She heard his voice but not the words, and she couldn't reply. She shook her hair back over her shoulders and then felt annoyed at herself. The man was staring at her impatiently but almost concerned.

His voice came over the glass partition again, now louder, "Can I help you?"

She said nothing and made sure she kept both arms tightly by her sides. She stared at the druggist and she felt like scratching her head, but she knew she shouldn't because she'd just thought of herself as a long rectangle, each of her arms part of a side. If she scratched her head the rectangle would collapse — there'd be a hole in it.

"That's a crazy thought," she said to herself, but she must have said it out loud because now he was leaning forward and saying, "I beg your pardon."

Thank God he hadn't heard her. Now she was scared. The pharmacist had left his cage and he was standing right beside her.

"Is there anything I can get you?"

She blurted out, "No!" and was startled by the sound of her voice.

The man wasn't offended. He smiled as if he was hoping she'd smile back, and said, "I'd be glad to help."

She wasn't sure what to make of him. Why was he smiling? It wasn't funny, her being there. Why didn't he leave her alone? Now she remembered him. John something, a few classes ahead of her in high school. Here he was, all graduated from pharmacy school and working in Simpson's drugstore! Once she had thought of working in a drugstore. She'd be in charge of the perfume. She could put it on free all day, while demonstrating it to the customers.

Rick hates perfume, she thought to herself as she turned to look for the perfume counter. But maybe that's it, maybe I came here to get some perfume, just for me. She felt better, surer. She straightened herself up and realized how bent over she had been. I'll be all right, she reassured herself. I *did* come here to get some perfume. Suddenly she was actually smiling.

"Some perfume."

"Any particular kind?" The clerk looked puzzled. What's the matter with him? John . . . John. . . . Oh, what's his last name? He shouldn't be here, anyway, selling perfume. He should be over there, with shaving cream and razors, or someplace else — in college still learning to be a pharmacist, back in his cage with those big bottles and prescriptions. Stop bothering me, stop trying to be helpful.

Abruptly she turned away from the clerk and looked down the aisle. A man stood near the door. He's around forty, probably in high school the same time my father was. He even looks like Daddy. They both look young for their age, but you can tell that they're not as young as they look. That tie he's wearing shows he's not young. Rick hates ties, but when he has to wear one — he gets dragged off to church some Sundays — he puts on the one I bought him. It's wide and full of color and he loves it. He even wears it sometimes when we go to a movie — on a tee shirt, as a joke, but also because he loves it.

Then John something-or-other was gone. He was up in the platform cage talking to another pharmacist. The two men stared at her. The older pharmacist moved toward the steps, then down the aisle toward her.

"Is anything wrong?"

Is anything wrong? "No," she heard herself saying. There's a lot wrong, she thought. Rick would say it right out if he were stoned and later on, he'd mimic the guy. If only she could be a mimic like Rick! He could imitate everyone, from the President on down. She could hear Rick's "Now let me make myself perfectly clear . . ." when suddenly the pharmacist's words penetrated: "Would you like me to call your parents?"

"No!" she said again and turned and ran out to the

street. They are such squares, those drugstore people, the straightest people in town, maybe even in all America. The ties they wear look like something President Franklin D. Roosevelt wore. When was he President, anyway? Rick heard him talk on a record his father has, and he imitates him, too.

Suddenly she felt sick and sweaty. The sun hurt her eyes. Her head drooped and she felt like crumbling to the sidewalk. She wasn't a puppet, she reminded herself. You have your own life to lead, her father had been telling her for the last year, two or three times a week lately. He meant that Rick was "leading her around."

Rick. She reached out for him, the name and *him*. It was his presence she wanted, and the reassurance that went with it. I wish we each had a spirit, like the Bible says, and we could send those spirits back and forth when we need help. Then I could send mine out to find Rick's.

The word jolted her — *help*. Those idiots in the drugstore wanted to "help." You have your own life to lead, she lectured herself. Maybe the best thing to do is call my father. No, the thought of him and his advice was too much, but in spite of herself, she was walking directly down the street toward home. There's nothing wrong with me, she told herself. Then she heard her father telling her, "There's nothing wrong with you, absolutely nothing."

That's the trouble, I feel like absolutely nothing. She stopped and felt a little dizzy.

"Watch out, girl, I'm getting ready to pull out!"

She'd been leaning on a Volkswagen. She bent over and looked in the window at a man of about fifty, bald, with glasses. He was looking at her half-scared and angry, as if she was another freaked-out kid making it hard for decent, sensible people to go about their business. She stared at him. "Look, kid, get off my car — please."

She didn't move.

"Do you want me to push you off?"

He started to open the door. Cathy bolted. As if the man couldn't stop himself, he continued to get out, then stood beside his car in the middle of traffic. "A real nut!" he yelled and slammed back into the car.

Once on her way, Cathy didn't stop. In ten minutes she was in sight of her house. By then the incident on

8

the street and the one in the drugstore were thoroughly out of her mind. As she turned into her driveway she was out of breath. Why did I run, she asked herself. Then, like a prosecuting attorney, she continued putting questions at herself: What am I doing, going home when it's a school day and I should be there? What if Mother is home? She could have decided to skip work just like I'm skipping school. What will the neighbors think if they see me? What if they tell my parents?

Was every neighbor on the street watching her? She looked at one door and then another, half preparing herself for each of them to swing open, revealing all her mother's "coffee club." Then she wondered whether the "coffee club" wasn't meeting in one of those houses at that very moment — which one? What would they think, seeing her out of school? I'm tired, she suddenly realized. But why? It's morning and I slept well last night.

She picked up a wagon left in her driveway by the boy next door. I may be tired, but I'm not lazy, she told herself. She threw it onto their lawn, but was surprised by how hard she had heaved the thing — it landed on their steps with a heavy thud. She expected ten women, her mother included, to come running out, calling her careless, inconsiderate, and a truant as well. Silence. The street seemed abandoned. Maybe this was the way it was after a tornado. Uncle Jim lives in Indiana, and he's always talking about tornadoes when he comes to visit, how everything is so quiet before and after them. The phone began to ring. She moved quickly toward the door. But something was wrong. For the first time she said to herself, something is wrong with me.

She groped in her pocket for her key. Where was it? The phone stopped but she felt no let-up. It was almost as if her head took over the phone's ringing, punishing her with its own ring. Come on, shape up, find that key, get into the house, go get your books, get over to school where you belong. I never took my keys, she said to herself as she tried to think back over the last hour or two. What to do? What's the matter? Why do I even want to go into the house?

She stood there. She could hear her mother and father speaking. "We don't like your attitude, Cathy." "There's going to have to be a change in your attitude." "Rick and you both have the same attitude." Just yesterday she'd heard that and she had cringed and shouted, "What is this business of *attitude* you're always talking about? Is there a person named *Attitude?*"

Her mother and father and sister just stared at her. Her sister laughed — it must be one of Cathy's jokes. Her father had put on his hurt look and asked what she meant. She hadn't answered, and fortunately the phone had rung. Cathy had quickly downed her supper, run upstairs and started crying. While the tears came and came, she tried to figure out what she *had* meant. Finally she had said out loud to herself, "I don't know." Now she again heard herself saying the same words. "I don't know."

She looked around. Somebody might be listening. But again, silence. Nobody was to be seen up and down the street. I've got to get in the house. I'm hungry. I'm tired. I'd like to sleep today, tonight, and maybe even tomorrow. I've never felt like this before. I'll be fine. It's just that Rick and I aren't getting along the way we used to. He'll help me. He *has* to. *Somebody* has to.

She didn't like what those last two thoughts did to her. She even felt herself trembling a little, but her mind said no, you're O.K., you're just "putting on a production." How many times in her life she'd heard that! She was "emotional," her father would say. "Stop putting on a production," he'd say. Go do this, go do that, go do what I want you to do. But even as she thought about her father she decided she was being unfair to him. He works hard. He loves Mother and me and Francie. Why am I thinking of him like that?

One "why" led to another. Why am I standing here, anyway? She felt people looking at her, urging her to stop dawdling, to open a window, climb into the house — and call a doctor. No, there weren't people looking at her. She was not a nut, she knew that. But she was tired. Rick was away and wouldn't be back for two days; she didn't want to see Jane and Margaret or any of her old friends. And she'd done something she'd never done before: stayed out of school.

She started running. She was in back of the house in a few seconds and the door there was unlocked. She leaped up the stairs, and threw herself on her bed. The man in the Volkswagen was printed on her mind as she buried her head in her pillow and waited for sleep to come. All I want is a rest, a long rest, twelve hours of sleep. Rick says he can go without sleep for two nights, then he needs twelve hours of it. I used to ask him why twelve, and he'd say it's a good number, one higher than eleven, everyone's lucky number. I need twelve lucky hours, then I'll be O.K. That man was still sitting in his Volkswagen. Suddenly his glasses began to change. They got bigger and turned into a woman's glasses — her homeroom teacher's. She pushed her head deeper in the pillow and tried to think of nothing, and for a few seconds she succeeded. She was too tired, her head wouldn't cooperate. She became conscious of the pillow — it wasn't soft like Francie's — and soon she was thinking of Rick, and wishing his head was beside hers on the pillow. Maybe it's because I miss him that I skipped school today? She came up with a few more maybe's. Maybe it's the cold weather. Maybe I'm getting sick — flu. Maybe it's my period coming, like Mother says. Maybe that's what's happening to me.

Her period was two weeks off. Maybe I'm speeding up, the cycle is going faster. Or maybe it's all the talk about next year: will you apply to college? Will you be planning to do something else? What? The junior year is the most important year in high school — that's what the teachers have been saying since we started, a month ago. She buried her head in the pillow again, *hard,* because there he was again, or there *she* was, it wasn't quite clear who. It was the man in the Volkswagen, but he was wearing her homeroom teacher's glasses and his voice was her teacher's, and she was talking about the junior year and all that.

A minute or so later Cathy jumped up from the bed. She started pacing up and down her room. She picked up her ruler and walked with it. If she could keep moving she could keep her mind clear. If she could walk back and forth she'd get even more tired and then she'd fall on that bed and go out like a light.

"That's what I want to do, go out like a light," she heard herself say. She repeated the words, and listened, feeling comforted by the sound of her own voice. She decided that she ought to do more of that. If she talked out loud to herself it might help her to settle down. So, she put the ruler down on her desk and paced and talked and tried to imagine that Rick was there, sitting on her bed, listening. "Don't you see, Rick, something is wrong. I don't know what it is. I'm just uptight, more than I've ever been. I can't figure out why. Everything seems to be going along fine. I'm not having any trouble in school. There's no real trouble here at home with my parents. Francie and I are friends besides being sisters. And you're great to me. I wish you weren't away now. I mean, I wish I could spend every second of my life with you, but we're not old enough to get married. Maybe we never will get married."

She stopped there. She looked hard at her bed, as if Rick *had* been there. She went over and sat down beside the spot where she'd imagined him being. For a moment she was going to reach out to him, but she stopped. Impatient with herself, she got up and resumed her pacing. Maybe if I kept a diary, she told herself, the way Rick's sister does, maybe then I could read over what I've written every week or so and figure out where I am. Rick says his sister analyzes herself; she's only fourteen but she does it. She told Rick she's her own shrink and Rick says it works. When she's feeling low, she writes in that notebook, and then she reads the stuff and tells Rick what's going on in her head. I used to think she was a real strange one, but maybe I'm getting a little odd myself.

She walked faster and spoke as if she had to get out a long, long speech and there were people waiting to hear her, and everyone there was anxious for her to get it over with. She spoke out loud, "I'm sixteen and not fourteen. I don't need any diary. There's nothing wrong with me, just a case of nerves because Rick went away for a few days to visit his grandmother and look at some colleges. You can't bring girl friends along to an interview. My parents don't approve of Rick anyway, because he's from a different 'background.' How different? We're not rich, but we're not poor. Rick's father has a lot of money. I'm not going out with Rick's father. What's the matter with *my* father, that's the thing I'm worried about — *my* father. And my mother, too. They both keep telling me I'm nervous. For a week I've heard that. All right, when they come home, I'll tell them that's why I stayed home today, because I needed a rest."

She sat down at her desk, picked up her red ballpoint pen and wrote the word "diary" on a piece of typing paper. She started making loops. It didn't take long for the word "diary" to disappear. She wrote "Rick," and then he became part of a big square. She couldn't write anything else. Instead she drew pictures, first of Rick's face, then of Francie, then of her father. She started to draw her mother, then she put the pen down. She threw the paper in the wastebasket, then picked it out and put it back on her desk. She got up and went to the window. She looked out, then realized she was staring. Somebody will see me, she told herself. *Who,* she answered back to herself, and what difference does it make? Why am I worried about every little thing that might happen?

She felt hungry. She had missed breakfast because she overslept. She'd run out of the house to get to school and instead had gone to the drugstore. Now her mind was back there. She had originally gone in to have some English muffins and milk, figuring a half hour or so would make no difference when she got to school. She could have been on a bus that broke down or something. She never did get her snack, she realized. Now she could, it would settle her down some. As she went downstairs she thought of eating scrambled eggs and muffins, and even the thought made her feel better. And she could hear Rick saying to her, You make the best scrambled eggs.

If only he were here! "That's what's wrong with me," she said and repeated out loud what she'd just thought, "if only he were here!"

As she broke the eggs and threw the shells in the wastebasket she began to have second thoughts. Maybe it wasn't only Rick's trip. She was lonely, but she'd been "nervous" at least four or five days before Rick left. And she'd started being nervous, she knew, even before Rick told her he was going away. Besides, he'd gone away with his family on weekends before and she hadn't minded. She even thought it was a good thing. They appreciated each other more when Monday came around.

The eggs were good. After eating them, Cathy went to school. She told her homeroom teacher that she had felt sick, but had recovered. Her teacher was touched that a student would return so promptly after an illness. "You still look sick," the teacher said, and Cathy could not forget that remark. I wasn't really sick, she firmly told herself. It proves how suggestible people are: you tell them something and they go right along with you. But now she began to wonder whether there wasn't something about her appearance and her state of mind that made her look sick.

Two days later Rick came back and Cathy was fine. She did ask him if he thought she looked sick, only to be told that she looked wonderful — especially wonderful after a separation of several days. Anyway, with Rick back she felt in good spirits and what had happened that morning she tucked away in her mind under the name of "panic." She must have freaked out because Rick had left and suddenly there was nothing to do that mattered and then everything became confused.

One afternoon she even went to the drugstore. She was with Rick and nothing, absolutely nothing, happened. She had found herself avoiding that store. The whole thing is silly, she had kept repeating to herself, and yet for some reason she had been afraid to go back. Now it was fine. In fact, she became practically euphoric, much to Rick's surprise and confusion. She felt she had to talk with him about what had happened because she was so convinced that whatever it was she had gone through would not repeat itself. She and Rick walked and talked and she tried to describe what she had experienced.

"Cathy, you're exaggerating. I'm sorry to say that, but I know you better than I know myself. You're as solid as anyone can be. You felt strange for a few minutes, so what. Everyone does sometimes. When I was away looking at colleges I felt strange. I'd wake up and I'd say to myself, What are you doing here? After a while all the people and places became a big blur. My father asked me about the people I saw at each place I visited and what the campus was like and I was tongue-tied. I was ashamed to tell him that I don't think the way he does. I couldn't remember every detail, every word, like he can."

Cathy glared at him but said nothing. Then she looked away, and a second later, she turned around.

"I want to go home."

"Cath, what's the matter?"

Cath — that was his ultimate weapon. She'd once told him so — how she dissolved when he called her that. "I'm all right. I'm just tired. We've been walking so far."

"We haven't walked more than a mile. You're not tired, you're upset, but I don't know why."

"I'm *not* upset. Please stop telling me what I am and how I feel."

"Come on, Cathy, let's stop this. Let's catch the bus. We can go to a good movie. The bus will take us right to the door."

"You go, Rick. I'll go home. I'll call you later."

"No, I don't want to leave you."

Something went wild in Cathy. Not that she *became* wild. She exercised perfect control over herself. If anything, she became icy and polite. She changed the subject and took control of the conversation. "I forgot something, Rick. I've got to get home soon, not right away, but soon. My mother and I are supposed to go shopping."

Rick went along with it. He stopped and looked in the window of a sporting goods shop, and she unaccountably felt relieved. She watched him for a second or two, then moved on by herself to the next window, a men's clothing store. She moved up close, so close that her nose touched the window. Time seemed to stop;

she stood there and looked, but she wasn't sure what she was looking at, or for how long. Her mind was elsewhere. She wished she was alone back home in her room. She jumped when Rick said her name.

She pulled away from the window as though the glass pushed her.

"Cath, I'm sorry if I've said something wrong. Let's go get a sandwich."

"Thank you, Rick; but I'm not hungry. I really would like to go home. I have to; my mother will be waiting."

They walked in silence. Cathy thought of humming, so she could make it clear that she was all right, was relaxed. But somehow the sound never came.

When she got home there was no one there, as she expected. She had been lying about her mother, something she was sure that Rick sensed, yet had felt helpless to challenge. Determined to avoid an argument, she had said a warm good-bye to him, but there was tension between them. I don't want a scene, I can't take a scene, she kept repeating to herself.

Now she was home she didn't know what to do. She walked from room to room. She sat down at the piano and touched a few keys. She wanted to play. If she could play she'd be all right. But she couldn't bring herself to do what she wanted so badly to do, even by ordering herself out loud to do it. "Play the piano, Cathy. Don't dawdle over it, play!" But she didn't touch a key.

Abruptly she got up and went to the kitchen. She wasn't hungry, but she thought she'd feel better if she ate something. When she saw the eggs in the refrigerator the whole thing began to come back — the horrible morning, the drugstore, the confusion in her room. Cooking eggs had made her feel better then. Maybe eggs were insurance against panic. What *is* the matter with me? Rick was right; I'm exaggerating. But I don't want him to see me like this. Like *what?* Why am I talking about *panic?* I'm not panicked. I wasn't panicked all last week. There's nothing bothering me — is there? Should I talk to anyone? What would I say? There's nothing to say, that's just the problem.

Tears, she felt tears in her eyes. Maybe if she just broke down and cried it would help. But she couldn't. She thought of onions: her eyes would fill up, and her troubles would wash away. She was still preoccupied.

That word "panic" kept crowding into her mind. I've used the word "panic" to myself, but I've never really felt panicky. I feel fine. There's absolutely nothing bothering me — so what is the trouble? She was annoyed with herself. Once when she had turned thirteen her father had taken her on his knees and spanked her. Later he had apologized, telling her she was too old for that. Now she had a picture in her mind of him spanking her, and then she saw herself spanking herself.

"I'm going upstairs." The sound of her voice startled her. She looked around. Was her mother home? Was Francie? Had anyone been watching her the last few minutes? Ridiculous — she knew she was alone. She started up the stairs and felt the beginning of a headache. I'll take some aspirin and sleep it off, she thought. As she entered her room she felt strangely sad. She had lived in that room for years, since she was five or six, as far back as she could remember. She looked around. The room looked as nice as ever. Her mother had never been able to stop cleaning up after her, and she loved her for doing it — even though at times she made all sorts of noises about not being a child any more and being able to look after herself. The rug had been vacuumed; its thousands of hairs were still upright. Her desk looked so neat, and her bed inviting with the small blanket lying there on top of the spread. What a lucky person I am, she thought — and then she remembered all the times her parents had yelled at her when she was younger and had done something wrong. Well, they were right, she insisted to herself, and her face became hard, as if she was ready to take on someone in an argument.

The headache was getting worse so she went for the aspirin. Shall I take one or two? She found herself swallowing three aspirin and then staring at the bottle. She wondered how many were inside. She quickly fastened the cover, put the bottle out of sight, and then threw herself on the bed. Why did I do that? This headache is no worse than any other. For a second there I thought of taking five or six. I have no patience anymore. I can't stand pain. I started crying yesterday just because I had a splinter in my hand.

As her mind raced on, her body seemed to relax for a moment. She stretched herself wide across the bed and looked up at the ceiling. The telephone rang and she got up to answer it, but went no further than the door of her room. She didn't want to talk with anyone. She thought of watching television. Perhaps that would distract her. But she rubbed her eyes and decided that they hurt. It was a bad headache and not going away, even with three aspirin. No use panicking, she told herself. This is just a bad headache and needs more than the usual number of aspirin. She pulled down the blinds. Her eyes really *did* hurt. For the hundredth time, she asked herself what was wrong — she was a high school junior doing well in school, from a nice comfortable family. She loved her parents and she and Francie weren't always fighting like some sisters. She'd gone to the doctor early in the summer, before working as a counselor in a camp, and he said she was in excellent health. She'd never been in a hospital in her life. Right now, all she had was a really bad headache, and nothing more.

But she wasn't convinced. Something made her restless. She found herself thinking of that druggist and the look on his face. She cringed and felt the impulse to run downstairs. "Ridiculous," she spoke out, and she had sounded so emphatic that she looked around. She must have been talking with someone! She shouldn't be alone, that's the mistake. Why did she turn Rick away — Rick, the one person she really trusted and depended upon? Was he right? What had *he* said that bothered her, or was she bothered anyway? The word lingered; she was bothered, *all bothered up,* as her grandmother used to put it.

She sat at her desk and looked at a geometry textbook. She opened it, flipped the pages, slammed it shut and was taken aback by the noise. As if to prove she could reverse things, she picked up the book again, turned the pages very slowly and gracefully and closed the book once again. That's better: not a sound! She began to poke around among her books. If only she could get her mind occupied! She wanted to read a book on psychology, but she had none available. Rick had offered to lend her one. No, she wasn't interested in "that stuff." That's what her father called subjects like psychology — "that stuff." He believed in a classical education; he'd had one — Latin and Greek — and he thought today's high school courses were "watered down." He had been pleased when she didn't take a course in "Human Growth and Development." It's all common sense, or if it isn't it's nonsense, he'd told her, and she had agreed.

Actually, she and Rick had argued about the psychology course. He felt he'd learned a lot in it. Cathy had echoed her father's words. "Your dad is a stuffed shirt," he'd told her, with a mixture of humor and earnestness. Both she and Rick realized how differently their families felt about things. Cathy's people were "square." And Rick's family was not, was socially more aware. Now Cathy wished she'd taken the course, or at least had a psychology book. But exactly what would she look up in a psychology book? Adolescent madness, melancholy — she tried a list of words beginning with "m."

She went over to the window and looked out. The street was quiet, empty. It used to be crowded at this time of the afternoon. There had been about a dozen of them, boys and girls, who had grown up together. Once, about seven years ago, they even organized themselves into the Golden Winners, named for their street, Golden Road. They had all wanted to buy shirts or sweaters with the club name on them but their parents had balked.

Suddenly Cathy felt quiet, at rest with herself. She recalled what it was like at breakfast when she had been eight or nine, the "arguments" with her sister over who gets what food first. She thought back to promotion days — when her mother had taken them to an ice cream parlor each year until they reached junior high. Often they had teamed up with some other kids and their parents. She thought of all those people, herself included, sitting in adjoining booths of the Evans Pharmacy and she felt like crying. The Evans Pharmacy was gone and the new drug store was farther away from home, bigger but with no ice cream. Evans Pharmacy used to have a blue sign, lit up at night, advertising its ice cream. She and all her friends knew the druggist. Sometimes he even gave them a free cone. Now, in the place where the store had been, there was a huge supermarket. It sells packaged ice cream.

You have to take a long ride to get served ice cream these days, she thought as she moved closer to the window. She felt its smooth, cool surface on her nose, her forehead. She wasn't looking outside, but looking back in time, thinking about Mr. Evans and his store and her friends. In a flash she scanned the street and it occurred to her that no one was there. All her friends were doing one thing or another, in one place or another. They all still lived near each other but had become parts of different worlds. Her mother had often said recently how sad the street seemed with practically no children anywhere to be seen. "Soon you'll all start marrying and we'll begin moving out to small apartments, and then young married couples will move in and it'll be like old times again."

Cathy could hear those words. She erased them by using her eyes. Across the street they needed to repave the driveway; next door the lawn was in bad shape; two doors down a shutter was dangling and that old, unregistered, abandoned car *still* hadn't been towed away to a junkyard. She'd been breathing onto the window and it was beginning to cloud up. She focused her eyes away from the street and onto the glass, hard. As a little girl she used to write on windows. Now she wrote on the clouded glass: CATHY. Then she wiped it away, and to make sure nothing was left, took a Kleenex from her desk and cleared the whole window. When that was done she pressed her forehead back against the glass.

The phone rang. She was sure it was Rick and she did not want to answer. Three rings and then silence. Wrong number. What if it had been Mother or Dad? What if they knew she were home and not answering the phone? Why didn't she want to answer the phone? The next question came loudly out of her mouth, "Please, tell me what's the matter with me." As she spoke those words, she turned her head until she faced not outside but down at her shoes. She examined them carefully: the left one looks better than the right and both are getting to the point where new soles and heels won't solve the problem. They are almost a year old. She eased herself out of each shoe and kicked them hard with her right foot clear across the room.

Now she stared at her feet, moving her toes and watching carefully. Suddenly, she was on her bed, her pillow over her head, clutching the sides of the mattress. "Oh!" was all she said. Through her mind a flash of images had passed — the druggist, Rick, and then a picture of herself lying on the lawn looking up at her window. It was broken and Cathy was terrified. She saw herself lying there, grinning at the sight of the smashed pane of glass. She continued to hold onto the mattress a minute or so longer, then released her grip, lifted the pillow and looked at the window. She smiled with relief at the sight of it, as intact as ever.

She needed aspirin. She must have a strange kind of headache disorder that was affecting her thinking. Maybe Dr. Strong could help. He had always talked to her apart from her mother, even when she was nine and sick in bed with viral pneumonia, and once, during a bad spell of vomiting and nausea. He didn't usually make home visits, but he'd grown up with her parents and liked them. She conjured up in her mind the sight of him, the sound of him, his manner, his presence, even his quirks, like saying "yes" a little too frequently, or always crossing his legs when he sat at the edge of the bed, and then moving his dangling foot around in a circle as he talked or listened or looked. She almost but not quite had the doctor speaking to her about her present condition. She pictured him all right, but he wasn't talking, only leaning over and smiling at her and questioning. Then he disappeared. There was no one there, nothing, only that window. I'm really O.K., she thought. I'm nervous; something is bothering me but I don't know what it is. I wish I'd just been in an automobile accident. I wish I'd been driving ninety-three miles an hour outside of some city a thousand miles from here, and I'd been hurt but not too badly, and the doctor called my parents and Rick and told them I'd be fine in a month or so. Then they would all want to fly out and I'd say no, absolutely not — because long-distance telephone calls are great fun.

She smiled at her own thoughts and pushed her hair back. She went into the bathroom and brushed it. But as she did so she saw herself in the mirror, and now for a few seconds she was leaning toward the mirror, pressing her face on it, feeling her spirits sag lower and lower. She dropped the brush, then felt herself kick it hard. She wondered about those aspirin. Should she take, maybe, five of them? *Then* would she feel better? Why not take *ten* of them? *All* of them? The bottle was only a quarter filled; she'd probably sleep for a day and a night, and then wake up cured.

The word "cured" stuck in her mind. She moved away from the bathroom mirror and grabbed onto a towel rack. Cured of *what,* she asked herself. Then in real desperation she ran to the phone. She'd call Dr.

Strong. Maybe he could come up with some advice. Maybe he'd tell her there's a virus going around and it affects your head. When she'd had pneumonia seven years earlier, he'd worried about her high fever. He'd told her not to worry if she felt a little jittery — that's what can happen. She told *him* not to worry. "My head won't splinter apart," she'd said, and the doctor had laughed. "Cathy, you're right," he'd said; "heads don't splinter so easily." If only it were then, not now, she wished with all her might. She picked up the phone book, looked up the doctor's number, started dialing, then said firmly, "no," as if she were scolding herself. She controlled an urge to slam down the phone; then she thought of pulling it out and throwing it. It surprised her. She ended up putting the phone down more softly than she'd ever done in her life.

She went back to pacing in her room, and for the first time thought to look at her watch. It's four-thirty — they'll be home soon. What do I do? Should I try to explain anything to them? I don't know how! I should get out of here. Should I call Rick? He's the only person in the world who really understands me. I mean, my parents want to, but they can't, not now.

34

She decided to leave immediately for Rick's house, not to call him. *If he's not there, I'll hide in the bushes and wait for him.*

That thought made her only more agitated. She hated Rick's parents. Even he called them snobs but she knew enough not to agree with him openly. She was secretly delighted when he sounded off against them and once, as he did so, she caught herself with a bit of a smile on her face. She knew Rick noticed — he saw her noticing him noticing it, and saw her, also, wiping it away all too quickly. After that he didn't talk too much about his parents, except when there was an argument to report, and she always tried to see their side, even if she really didn't. "You don't have to say that," he'd tell her — but he had to because she was afraid. It bothered her that he couldn't just forget his parents' criticism when he was with her — that he had to fight them in front of her, even after that incident.

I can't go there, she decided. *They'd see me. They'd* catch *me* — it would come to that. They have those two awful dogs — sweet-sounding names, Huckleberry and Bianca, but noisy and fiercely loyal to Rick's father and, she always feared, ready to lunge at anyone he pointed at after snapping his fingers. She'd thought of poisoning them; she had told Rick her idea: slow doses of arsenic or something, like in a movie. She'd never approached that house without Rick and she was sure she couldn't now.

So, the phone. She called him up and the maid answered. She hung up instantly. She was furious with herself, and confused, and finally, quite scared. She spoke out loud again: "I can't even call up my boyfriend, and if I did, I wouldn't know what to say — where to begin and how to tell him what's on my mind. Even if I *did* get Dr. Strong what would I say to *him?*" She was back on the bed — again wishing that she could break into tears and sob away everything wrong with her, but her eyes were dry.

As she lay there she decided she was sick, with a germ or virus or something like that. She went back to the bathroom and got the thermometer, put it in her mouth, and briefly glanced at herself once more in the mirror. She became a little too aware of the presence of the thermometer — not of how she looked with it in her mouth, but how it felt under her tongue and between her teeth. She could bite it. She'd probably end

up swallowing the mercury and maybe some glass —
and then she really *would* need to go to Dr. Strong.
She went back to the bed and waited for three minutes,
thinking mostly about how wonderful it would be if
she had a fever of 102° or 103°. She felt relaxed as
soon as the thermometer was out of her mouth, but
she wouldn't look at it right away. She got up and put
it on her bureau. She paced back and forth. She had an
urge to smash the thermometer. She went back to the
bureau to get it, was wonderfully gentle with it. She
rubbed her finger down it and looked: a little over 97°.
She was disappointed, but her mind was agile. It's
below normal, by more than a degree, she thought.
Then she had another idea: maybe she could put the
thermometer on the light bulb for a split second and
the mercury would go way up, and then when her
mother came home she could show her the thermometer, and they'd take her to Dr. Strong. She reminded
herself that if her mother put her hand on her forehead, as she always did in such circumstances, the
plan would fail. But there were always hot towels to
make her head feel warm and sweaty.

Abruptly she lost interest in the whole subject —

fevers, a trick to get to the doctor's. You are being a silly, melodramatic baby, she sternly lectured herself. She remembered a math teacher calling a classmate of hers "a melodramatic little girl who should be spanked." She sat down at the edge of the bed and in her mind tried to summarize for herself what had been going on. There was that strange episode in the drugstore and the man outside with the Volkswagen. There was some tension between her and Rick when he came back — though not much, really. But most of all there were these peculiar thoughts and urges she was having, which she couldn't understand, couldn't put into words. She began to realize that even if Dr. Strong were right there in her room and there was no one else there to inhibit her, she'd be at a loss to explain exactly what it was that made her feel she ought to talk with him.

She gently slapped her knee, as if to give herself a bit of a spanking, and resolved to go out and pull some weeds and help straighten out the garage — so filled up with things the car had to stay out on the street. And she got herself to do just that. She said to herself that she must. She *willed* herself outside and *willed* herself to work. All the while, as she was on her knees plucking weeds, she was conscious of her need to keep an eye on herself, keep pushing at herself to do the task before her. She began to believe that this was the way she'd have to live the rest of her life — taking each step deliberately, consciously, or rather, self-consciously.

Cathy spent the next hour pulling or dragging junk together and putting it all in green plastic bags. Maybe this is what doctors would call "therapeutic jobs," thought Cathy. Whether or not, she was more nearly herself by the time her parents and sister came home. She lost her calm for a few minutes but became increasingly self-confident when she realized that the "act" she was putting on for their benefit was working very well. And that night she had a perfect excuse to retire to her room early, and indeed her parents were exceptionally solicitous because her burst of energy at the expense of some weeds and some well-established debris had obviously cost something. It deserved any and every kind of recognition because Cathy and her sister had never been required to do chores outside the house.

Then Cathy's father made an unfortunate mistake in expressing his gratitude. "So many people of your age are self-centered; they wouldn't dream of thinking of others — of going out and doing what you did, Cathy." He had meant to be complimentary — extolling his daughter at the expense of a large, nondescript horde of youths of her age. Instead he had hurt her.

What a stupid way to talk, she thought. He is so blind about young people — so prejudicial, so stupid. She had all she could do to control her feelings of shame and anger and that phrase, "self-centered," made her uneasy. She kept thinking of it as she sat at the table. Trouble makes us self-centered. Perhaps she was more self-centered than any of those her father was so busily engaged in condemning. No one could be more worried about herself than she had recently been. Feeling that way, feeling under that kind of pressure, how long could her effort to keep her "cool" last?

That night she slept well and next morning she woke up in good spirits. It was raining. She noticed that fact a little too carefully — would bad weather produce another "mood"? But she felt so well that soon the weather was forgotten. She put on a blouse

Rick liked, and spent most of the next hour or so thinking about him. What was going to happen between them? Why hadn't she ever gone out with anyone else more than once? Rick would be away in college next year, would that be the end of their friendship? What would she do the year after that? She didn't really care about college. She wasn't a particularly good student and her parents had barely enough money, in her father's words, "to keep the finance people away." She went from one question to the other, phrasing and rephrasing them so that by implication she could consider their answers. With him away in college, won't I definitely lose him? With him away in college what kind of problems will I have to struggle with? With him away in college — oh God, what will it be like?

The last question almost sent her spinning, dizzied by all the forces at work within her. But she rallied and went off to school, telling herself on the bus that she would, if necessary, call Dr. Strong and ask him for some strong scouring soap for the mind. She arrived at school feeling as if she had already taken that soap, and indeed it had worked one hundred percent.

That day's tension was familiar — when would she

see Rick? They did meet and they got along well, and after school it was even better. Rick seemed to see nothing wrong with her. She watched him, even girded herself for the expected solicitousness. He was always so exceptionally thoughtful, so considerate. He was natural and relaxed with her, and she knew him well enough to spot any deception. As they walked home that day, she noticed a building with a lot of doctors' names on it and she thought to herself, I won't have to see Dr. Strong. I wouldn't mind being a doctor or a nurse myself. After yesterday and last week, I'd know what patients meant if they came in and said they didn't know what's the matter with them, but they really felt mixed-up, with all sorts of funny ideas running through their heads.

The next day and the day after that did not bring back those "funny ideas." Then, weeks later, at the supper table her father asked a question. "Have you given any thought to what you might want to do after high school?" It was a not uncommon question to put to a sixteen-year-old nearing seventeen. It was worded so very tactfully and tentatively by her father that Cathy could scarcely feel under any pressure to come up with a reply unless she herself felt like talking about her "future." She answered him immediately and casually, "Oh, Dad, I guess I have a little time to come up with something." Her father agreed, and nothing more was said. Cathy enjoyed the rest of the dinner, in fact complimented her mother on the really delicious home-made soup and the blueberry pie. As they disbanded from the table and all marched toward the television set to look at the evening news, Cathy suddenly felt the urge to break ranks.

"I've got a little extra work to do. I think I'll go right upstairs and get a start on it."

She meant what she said, too. The work was getting harder, especially the math, which she disliked and never did well in. But when she got upstairs and into her room it was as if the world was suddenly coming to an end and Judgment Day would arrive tomorrow at the very latest. She ran for the bed and lay on her stomach and stretched her legs and her arms out and pressed her face so hard into the spread that she felt its pattern printed on her skin. She seemed to be back where she left off weeks and weeks ago. She wanted to cry, but couldn't. Now she was utterly absorbed with that dilemma. Why couldn't she cry? If only she could cry, she'd rid herself, she felt sure, of the terrible influence that kept cropping up, something she could recognize but not understand.

It was back. I'm panicked again, she said to herself, not calmly but with the assurance a person feels when she knows how to name something formerly indefinable.

So it was that Cathy lay there wondering not when this "attack," as she now thought of it, would end, but when and under what circumstances she might expect the next one to occur. She realized, as she recalled the previous incidents, that there was simply no rhyme or reason to all of this — or none *she* could figure out. She felt her mind torn in two. Part of it caught with "panic" and urging her, as though she were a horse and it a whip, to race around the room, run out of the house, call the doctor, try taking her temperature. Another part was telling her that she'd survived so far, and this "beginning of an attack," as she was by then thinking of it, didn't seem as bad as the others had been.

In fact, she was right. She lay there for about an

hour, got up from the bed considerably quieter, and went to her desk. She felt a headache and decided to risk a worsening of the spell by going for some aspirin. She managed, by watching over herself carefully and urging herself on, to take two aspirin and get out of the bathroom in pretty good shape — no wild thoughts, no ideas of swallowing large numbers of pills, no staring at herself, no throwing objects around. Back on her bed, she waited for the headache to yield to the power of those two small white tablets. She pictured the aspirin going through her body, from her stomach up toward her brain, and wondered if her parents were watching on television the same diagram she conjured up in her mind. She felt twinges of excitement. She wanted to jump up and run someplace, do something, hurl something toward the window. But she was able to keep herself on the bed, and she considered that a significant achievement. She was even able to think about herself with some detachment, despite the fact that she was struggling to keep herself quiet and as calm as she could possibly be.

She thought of certain programs, serials on television or movies about mental patients and their psychiatrists. She decided she really did have some kind of psychological hangup but couldn't figure out what kind. She tried classifying psychiatric diseases, trying to find her own. She wasn't out of her mind, making no sense or bad sense; she didn't have some terrible fear of heights or tunnels or the dark. She had a friend who really did get hysterical when she looked down from a skyscraper and so wouldn't go near them, who wouldn't climb a ladder or even a tree. Cathy wasn't like that. She wasn't moping around the house unable to do things or meet people, nor was she in trouble with the law like a few kids at school who were seeing psychiatrists after taking drugs or stealing cars.

Her mind was superactive, *racing*. Something was happening inside that made her feel restless and vulnerable. She saw too much, remembered too much, noticed things she usually overlooked. Things and people aroused her for no good reason — that man in the Volkswagen, for instance, or the druggist. *My body and my head start jumping as if I've touched a live wire. I'm all heated up, charged up, and I start zigzagging wildly from one thing to another and then suddenly it's over. I can be myself again. If I knew for sure I had to go through this a few times a year I would try to sit back and learn to take it, but what if they come more often?*

Cathy knew she was in trouble. I need someone to talk with, a good doctor, perhaps, but I'm not crazy. Even saying that to herself was a relief, not because she knew she was right and not because she was whistling in the dark, gaining cheap comfort. It was just that she felt enough in control to describe herself and what she had gone through. She knew what to expect — or so she hoped.

A week later Cathy was more worried. The premonitions came three or four times a day. If she went to this store or that classroom, if she didn't do one thing before another, she'd experience the start of an "attack." She would feel nervous and start noticing somebody too closely. She was becoming cautious about her daily schedule, about where she walked and precisely when she arrived at school. Then Rick got concerned and she laughed at him. It was a brave laugh and he didn't press the point, but his expression of concern was a devastating blow. She minded it almost more than the attacks themselves.

That night she couldn't sleep. She went to bed feeling tired and fell asleep but an hour later she was awake. Nothing would put her back to sleep, not two aspirin nor warm milk, not a snack, not her radio playing softly, not any possible arrangement she could imagine — with two pillows, with one, with none, with a blanket, without one, even with her head at the foot of the bed.

The insomnia continued two, three nights.

All the while she lay awake she thought more and more about herself. Would an attack come on? Why wasn't one coming on? Who could she tell about it? Who would understand?

She wished she were afraid of dogs, like her sister. She wished some dog had suddenly run into that drugstore weeks and weeks ago (by now she had lived with those episodes long enough to feel it had been a matter of years) and run toward her and bit her. Then she would have been terrified, and everyone would understand why. If she woke up at midnight screaming loudly enough to wake up the entire neighborhood, even if she woke up barking like a dog, everyone would be considerate and understanding. She conjured up all sorts of pictures: Rick's awful dogs arriving in that drugstore, attacking the druggist, gobbling up a lot of his pills, going after her next but dropping dead just as they got to her legs — poisoned (at last!) by their indiscriminate greed. She knew she wasn't going to have an attack when she could lie there in bed at two or three in the morning and think of that mean-faced, flinty-eyed man in the Volkswagen, or those two ridiculous, annoying, awful dogs of Rick's, and still not get upset.

Maybe all her troubles would come to this — anguish through the night, tossing and turning, long stretches of thinking followed by grim attempts to keep everything, absolutely everything, out of her mind.

What would she do at breakfast? How would she look? What would her parents say if she appeared with huge circles around her eyes? Anyway what *are* those circles that you read about? What causes them? Do they appear after a few nights of insomnia? Does it take a week or two or even more?

She did fall asleep, but very briefly indeed. At four A.M. she had checked her watch. The next thing she knew she was grabbing at the table beside her bed, trying to find her clock, and bumping into the lamp and a couple of magazines. There it was. Her arm had swung wide, as if she were casting a net, and in it came — with its luminescent news: 4:35.

"I don't believe it," she said aloud. "I just don't believe it." Silence. Maybe she was back asleep. But no, she was engrossed in thinking about the dream she'd had during that thirty-five-minute interlude of unconsciousness, if not sleep.

It took her a few minutes to recover the dream. She cast about in her mind, groping for a detail, losing it, remembering nothing, and then, all of a sudden, as with the clock, she had it. That druggist and his mortar and pestle, he was grinding something up and there were a lot of people looking, including herself and Rick. No one knew what it was and everyone wanted to know — but the druggist would say nothing. He just stood there pounding away, looking up for a second now and then at those watching him. End of scene. Then there was another hard-to-understand part of the dream. Rick was living in a tent, maybe even an Indian tepee. He sat there in front of the place, smoking a pipe but not a regular pipe like the kind her father used. It was a much longer kind, which was why she thought he was pretending to be an Indian. She came up and asked him if she could join him and he said, yes, and motioned to her to sit down beside him. She did. He gave her the pipe but she wasn't sure she should use it. Then a big car started coming toward them, a limousine with two American flags, one on each front fender. She couldn't make out the people inside, but Rick said they were the enemy and she agreed. He refused to move. She sat still at his side. The car drew closer and closer. She was sure that car meant to run right into them, kill them, demolish the tent, then move onto the next target. As it got up close she could see the driver, a man who wore a chauffeur's uniform. There were other people in the back. Sun-glare turned the car into a big blur and finally, just before it was on top of them, Rick and she leapt to safety — and she woke up.

She wasn't terrified in the dream or afterward when she thought about it, even though she had faced an unfriendly collection of people who seemed intent on killing Rick and her. The dream simply puzzled her. The dream struck her as exceptionally vivid and persistent. She practically never dreamed. Yes, sometimes in the morning she knew something had been going on up there in her head during the night. Brushing her teeth or dressing, she'd think a little story in her mind — the family had gone on a trip, and x happened or y did — and she'd say to herself, that's what a dream is like.

Slowly she sat up in bed and pushed away the quilt. She got up, now slightly upset but not about to go into any panic. My body is tired, she thought, but my mind isn't. She stretched, trying to relax herself. What is going on in that head of mine?

She watched the morning come. The birds, a virtual alarm clock of them, and an ever so subtle change in the night were followed by the franker intrusion of daylight, and eventually one more defeat for darkness. She hated to see the dawn turn into morning. For some inexplicable reason it really was a loss. She knew she had to wash, to dress, and try to look as if she had slept all night. What if someone told her she looked as if she hadn't slept? Did she look like an insomniac in a television ad? Would she dare go to school and risk falling asleep there? Already, as she brushed her teeth and got ready to take a shower, she felt as if, at last, she could go to bed and "conk out" for twenty-four hours. And what about Dr. Strong — hadn't the time come to go see him? She knew how she'd begin: I can't sleep the way I used to. Then she'd tell him the rest, though she still wasn't sure how to put it all in words.

In the shower she melted under the warm water. Cold water changed that. She came out ready to go, and ready to put on a bit of a show. She almost succeeded, too, because her father told her how great she looked. Her mother agreed. It was only when she was putting her coat on that she felt her guard go, and then only because she thought she was alone in the hall. She looked in the mirror. There weren't any black circles around her eyes, yet she felt she radiated nothing but exhaustion and weariness. She tried to smile and couldn't. It was almost as if her face muscles were too tired to go along with her mind's will. Then she yawned, not once but three long, full times. Her father had been watching from the dining room doorway. "Cathy, for a girl who looks so lovely this morning, you seem awfully sleepy. What's the matter?"

She was hurt, annoyed, worried. She also felt herself

oddly weak and unable to respond, ironic in view of her success at the breakfast table. Quick, what to reply? She felt like a horse who has done all she can and done it well, now being flogged for the last time to get over one final hurdle, but not quite able to do the job. She called upon herself, warned herself, but she was unable to speak a single word. All she needed to do, she knew, was smile a little and agree with her father and light-heartedly bid him good-bye. That would be that. But she failed the test.

Even as he came closer and said, "Cathy, is everything all right?" she knew she could rescue herself. She remained silent. My voice is as tired as the rest of me, she thought.

"Cathy, are you sure there's nothing wrong?" Now her father was right beside her, and she looked up at him. There were his gray eyes, so cool yet inviting, and that one small scar on his forehead.

It was his hand on her shoulder that did it. She whirled around, threw herself into his arms and began to cry. Her mother and Francie came running into the hall. He waved them away and stood there holding her. Cathy tried to speak, but could only blurt out,

"I'm sorry." He didn't encourage her to speak. After a minute or so her sobs slowed and stopped. "I was afraid if I started to cry I'd never stop. But I did."

"Can we do anything to help you, Cathy?"

"Oh, Dad, it's just more complicated and crazy than I can begin to tell you. I don't even know *how* to begin, what to say. All I know is that I didn't get much sleep last night and I'm afraid to go to school today. I think I'd walk into that math class, sit down, and they'd have to carry me out on a stretcher, because in a minute I'd be asleep and I'd never wake up on my own."

Her mother's face was tense with worry. She stood with her back pressed tightly against the hall closet door and said, "Cathy, that's not like you, not sleeping. What's bothering you?"

"Oh, Mom, I wish I could tell you something *specific*. That's the trouble, there isn't anything special. I wish I could just start screaming, or pulling my hair out or something. Then I could be tied up and carried over to Dr. Strong."

"Cathy, don't talk like that!" Francie looked frightened. "Mother, shouldn't I stay home from school and stay with Cathy?"

"No, you go on. If you stay longer you'll miss your bus. We'll manage. Cathy will be all right."

Her mother and Francie moved toward the front door and Cathy followed them. Cathy hugged her sister and said, "I'm O.K. I really am. Don't worry." Then, just before closing the door she said, "Please try to find Rick and tell him I've got a cold or something, and just couldn't get up this morning. Don't tell him I was tossing and turning last night. He'll worry. Ask him if he'll call me later." Then she felt the tears coming again but she choked them back.

She sat on a chair across from her parents, who sat together on the living room couch. Their faces were frightened and helpless. She didn't want to be secretive or independent. She was honestly unable to put into words all those strange feelings and impulses. She sat there on the scratchy couch trying to describe her "bad phase or something," trying to tell them that if the thoughts and impulses had only been worse she might be having an easier time of it.

She stumbled over her words, tried to convey how suddenly "strange" she had felt in the drugstore, on the street walking with Rick, in her own room, by day and by night. She assured her parents there was nothing serious the matter with her, that Rick and she were getting on fine, that there was nothing she was holding back from them. She wanted them to know how trapped she felt.

"I get this feeling inside and it takes over for me. I look at things too hard. I think people are watching me."

Her parents made reassuring noises, but Cathy had already used on herself all the comforting words they offered. As she listened to them she felt tears pushing into her eyes and then, all of a sudden, she felt a surge of anger. There they were, looking at her. Looking, looking, looking. Her mother was trying to be nice; her father was not quite sure whether to shout at her or to be understanding. Cathy's whole life seemed wrapped up in them: her mother always trying to keep things going, making peace if any argument came up, and her father always holding back for a while until he was sure, until he knew which of his several sermons to deliver. I've had enough of this, she thought. I've had enough of *them*. I'd like to scream. I'd like to run out of this house and never come back.

She saw herself running. She pictured herself with a glass of water, throwing it at the wall, just missing one of her parents. Then tears blinded her before she even knew she felt like crying. Actually, she *didn't* feel like crying. She hit her one hand with the other, the fist into the palm, over and over again. Finally she screamed: "Leave me alone. The both of you, leave me alone. I'm tired of your questions, your pats on the back, your 'there, there, everything will be O.K.'" And she kicked the chair she'd been sitting on and ran out of the room and upstairs, shouting, "I've got to get out of here, I've got to."

That afternoon Cathy and her mother went to see Dr. Strong. Cathy had indeed fallen asleep in the morning. Her mother had called the office where she worked to say she had to stay home with her sick daughter. Cathy had wanted little lunch, and her mother, already puzzled by her daughter's sudden emergence into psychological trouble, felt a glimmer of old-fashioned hope. The child was not eating correctly and no wonder she became emotional and confused and tired and sleepless and all the rest. After Cathy had turned down tomato bisque soup and crackers, and the offer of any other soup in the cupboard, and had refused a bacon, lettuce and tomato sandwich or a ham and cheese one, either, her mother lost her patience.

"Cathy, I wish you'd eat something. A cup of tea and a Ritz cracker isn't a lunch; it isn't even a snack. I know, you don't feel well but you've got to keep your strength up. When I'm not eating well, it affects my mind. I lose my energy and I start getting morbid and . . ." Cathy got up and headed toward the door.

"Cathy! Please tell me what is bothering you. Where are you going?"

"Mother, I am not morbid and you've never been morbid in your life. Let's stop talking about what I should eat and what your dieting does to your head. I'm about five pounds overweight; not a lot, but enough for me to spare a few meals. I'm just not hungry and that's that."

"All right. I didn't mean to push you. I'm just worried, Cathy."

"I am, too, Mother! I'm falling apart. It isn't just the sleep I lost last night. It's these crazy thoughts. I want to run, run, run, or swallow a lot of aspirin. I'm *not* going to do it. I haven't the slightest intention of hurting myself. It's just that funny ideas cross my head and they never used to at all, never, until a month or so ago. Why? That's what I want to know." She started to cry again, quietly.

Her mother glanced at her watch, came and hugged her, took a handkerchief and wiped her face. "It's time to go to the doctor's."

They sat in Dr. Strong's waiting room and turned the pages of old copies of *Time* and *Life*. Cathy had read many of the magazines before but she leafed through them, reread this or that, and managed to accomplish her purpose, keeping her mind off herself. Her mother was less successful. She picked up and put down magazines in such rapid succession she had to say out loud to Cathy, "I'm no great reader." Reassuringly, Cathy replied: "Mother, you just like to read at the end of the day when everything is quiet and everything's done."

"You're right, Cathy." And that was all they said to each other until Dr. Strong came in from outside, a little out of breath, full of apologies, and asking for "one minute" so that he could put the black bag he was carrying in his office, make a telephone call, and settle down for his afternoon of office patients, of which Cathy was to be the first. "Hospitals are places that make you late," he said, disappearing behind the door to his examining room.

When Cathy finally got into his office, she didn't know how to begin. She fumbled with a few remarks about not sleeping well and eating poorly and he nodded seriously. She was beginning to be at a loss for words when he took over. "How old are you, Cathy? Excuse me for forgetting."

"I'm sixteen, just had my birthday three months ago."

"What year are you in high school?"

"Finishing up my junior year. I'll be a senior this fall."

"Oh! Time sure does fly. I can remember you when you were a little girl. I almost delivered you, in fact. The obstetrician was away for a day or two and I'd agreed to back him up. But you were only sending out preliminary warnings, it turned out. We had to be ready, because you came out walking. Know what that means?"

"No, Doctor, I don't think so."

"Hasn't your mother told you that you were a breech delivery? That means your feet came out first, not your head. It's a relatively small minority of children who are born that way. Not that it makes any difference in the long run, so long as you're born healthy, and you surely were. I saw you a few minutes after you were delivered and you were active and had a good, loud cry. I told your mother she had a girl just vibrating with good health and spirits. She'd been worried because you were a little overdue, but I said that just shows good common sense. It's a tough world to come into."

They seemed nearer the subject to be discussed. Cathy squirmed a little in the leather chair, uncrossed her legs, then crossed them again. Dr. Strong was asking her questions, vaguely medical questions. "How's your dad doing? How's your mother's bad knee?" She in turn was replying with as much accuracy as she knew how, but she was aware that time was running out. Even as she talked, she felt distant from her own words and preoccupied with the next and immediately up-coming phase of her visit with this kind man. Within seconds, though, she had no time for further casual talk and semidetached apprehensiveness.

"Tell me, Cathy, what is troubling you, beyond the occasional bouts of sleeplessness and indifference to food?" Silence. She stretched out her hand, as if she were going to point at someone or something, or per-haps illustrate her words. But the words were not com-ing, in spite of that gesture. She looked away from the doctor then back to him. He wasn't going to let her nervousness and the failure of her speech overwhelm her. He started asking her another series of questions based on his clinical intuition and experience.

"Is it some pain you're having in your body, some-thing not working quite well? Or is something worry-ing you or puzzling you? I'd like to be of help. I know how hard it is to talk about some of these things. I'll keep asking questions if you wish, but can you tell me what's wrong?"

She began talking and half-listening to herself, and seeing the encouragement in Dr. Strong's manner, she decided her mind was working well enough to continue. "I think there's something wrong up in my head. I've had attacks. I mean, I don't know what to call them, but I feel myself overwhelmed. People seem to be looking at me, or criticizing me, or I'll have funny thoughts crossing my mind." She stopped.

"Cathy, could you tell me what some of those thoughts are?"

She resumed her monologue more confidently. She tried to give the doctor a faithful account of those episodes, especially the one in the drugstore. Dr. Strong listened. For about half an hour Cathy described her recent difficulties and toward the end, after she had more or less conveyed all she knew to say, there was an abrupt turn in her comments — away from description and toward severe self-criticism. "I don't know what you can make of all this. My parents are wonderful, and they've given me and my sister so much. We have a nice house and each of us has our own room. Daddy can't afford fancy colleges but he said he'd take on a second job and Mother would work extra hours, if I wanted to try to get a partial scholarship someplace. I doubt I can. I'm not much of a student. Rick is. And he sure doesn't need any scholarship. And here I am 'messing up,' like Dad used to say when we were younger and we didn't do an errand the way he asked us to. Maybe what I need is a good old-fashioned spanking. Rick says his father gets angry at him and tells him he needs a good swift kick in the pants. Maybe that's what I need."

"Why, Cathy? You've been having some upsetting experiences. You have a right to seek help without blaming yourself for anything. Anyway, will you let me do a little talking now?"

Cathy was relieved to do so.

"I'm not a psychiatrist, as you know, Cathy. The time was when I'd have to begin a talk like this by explaining to you what a psychiatrist is, and how they do their work. Not any more. Psychiatrists are everywhere, on all kinds of television programs and in the movies. They are familiar to your generation, even if they are made fun of, certainly more so than to mine. I don't practice psychiatry but I've spent a lot of time with young people, listening to them and just plain watching them grow up. It's a satisfying job, let me tell you.

"Now, I think I'm sure of this. Your mind has been

going through some shifts, that's what I like to call them. It's like with a car, you shift gears at certain points, and you can feel it. Or with a bicycle. My son has a ten-speed racing bike and it's hard work figuring out which of those two gears should be where. I'm not trying to make light of what you've gone through. I just want to emphasize what you have pointed out. You are getting ready to go into your last year of high school, your boyfriend is graduating and leaving for college, and you don't quite know where you want to go or what you want to do. All that is natural for someone your age, and none of it is a justifiable cause for a spanking or kick in the pants. Even though you keep telling me that you haven't been under any special pressure, I can see plenty of reason. You've been very close to one, and only one, boy for three or four years, and now the whole high school world is coming to an end for both of you. Next year, even though you'll be there, and a senior with all the advantages of being one, Rick will be gone. And apart from Rick, there's your own life facing you. Should you try to become a nurse, as you once mentioned you might want to be, or go to a secretarial school or get a job or try to save money and go to college someday? I don't know how to advise you on all that, though I'm willing to try. I *do* know that you have good cause to be more than a little worried and preoccupied. Now as to your mind, let me try to give you my reactions to what I've heard. Would you let me do that?"

Cathy felt tears coming to her eyes. Because he was making her thoughts make sense, she should cry? She hurriedly said, "Yes." She certainly couldn't talk now. "O.K.," he replied, and took a sip of water.

"The mind," he began, "picks up messages from the outside world as well as from inside us. When I'm in a good mood, I pick and choose from the weather and the news to substantiate my good mood. When I feel lousy, I pick up the bad even on the best day. Needless to say, there's always plenty of trouble in the world to make my melancholy seem like the most sensible and justifiable thing in the world. What you've been telling me, and you've done a better job than you give yourself credit for, might be put like this. 'Doctor, I haven't been feeling well lately. I'm reaching a critical point in my life. My boyfriend is going to be graduating and leaving here, leaving me! He'll be gone in a few months and next year at this time I'll be more on my own than ever before. I guess I'll be lonely and I'll be under some pressure to build a whole new world for myself. So, what does my mind go and do to me? Well, it starts sending signals that it recognizes what's up ahead, around a few bends of the road, and maybe by sending those signals it's preparing itself for the worst and hoping to make the worst not so bad, after all.' "

He paused as if to make sure that Cathy understood. She didn't say anything, just smiled faintly out of nervousness and to show she was listening. "Now," he asked, "I wonder whether you think I'm on the right track?"

Cathy felt he was. She was certainly aware that she was in her junior year, and Rick had been interviewed at various colleges and expected to hear from them soon. But she had some intelligent reservations to express and she did so with more assurance than she had shown earlier when she tried to describe her problems. "What I don't understand is why I should be getting these strange thoughts and these sudden ideas to bite the thermometer or run away or hit my head against the window. I'm scared that I'm going crazy. A lot of people get lonely. I'm not the only girl who's been going steady with a boy who's graduating. He may decide he wants to play the field in college and I wouldn't really blame Rick. What about all the other kids in my class? Are they as confused as I am? A lot of them have given less thought to what they might do next year, or the year after, than I have. Why aren't they as scared of themselves as I am?"

She stopped and looked at Dr. Strong. Had he heard what she said? And the funny way she put it? "Why aren't they as scared of themselves as I am." The doctor seemed to want her to continue. "What I just said, Doctor — about being scared of myself — that's the problem, that's why I'm here. I've felt low but I've never before been frightened of my own mind. It's really given me a rough time the last few weeks. I mean, it's played tricks, teased me, and once or twice really frightened me. And I never know when it's going to happen. Tomorrow, out of the clear blue sky, I could be shopping or walking or just sitting at home, and all of a sudden, it might happen. There's no telling how long it will last or what I can do to snap out of it. Even in the middle of the attack, I know I'm freaked out but I can't stop it. A few times I've felt like rushing into the street, even pulling a fire alarm and asking the firemen, when they come, to take me away and lock me up. If there'd been a policeman in the drugstore that day, I would have turned myself in. It's all me. It's not one hundred percent right me versus one hundred percent wrong everyone else. It's my head, it's . . ."

The doctor interrupted. "I know, Cathy. If anything, you're *too* willing to share the blame with others. No one could accuse you of sparing yourself."

That remark made her squirm. Why did he have to say that? She was trying to describe how she felt, and he was trying to be nice to her. She felt herself even getting angry at him. The result was paralysis. She couldn't say another word. He repeated himself in a slightly different way. She became even more angry and felt herself grow hot and restless. He offered her water and she shook her head, then lowered it, looking into her lap. He asked her what was wrong. She didn't raise her head. She couldn't, even though she wanted to.

"Cathy," he said firmly, "this isn't easy, talking to someone about what's going on in your head. We all want privacy; no one wants others poking into their secret wishes and fears. When we get to be twelve or thirteen we don't want even our mothers and fathers doing that. I find it the most difficult part of my work, though you'd be surprised at how much I have to be a kind of advisor or special friend. Not only with young people. I read in a medical journal a month or two ago that about a half to two thirds of the patients seen by a general practitioner like me, a regular doc who doesn't specialize in psychiatry, are people who basically are troubled and unhappy because of their emotions, their thinking and feelings. Now they may have real physical complaints, but their main problem is fears, irritations, envies, loneliness, frustrations, and on and on.

"I know. As I list off all the ordinary psychological troubles human beings have, you begin to wonder how any of us survive. But the mind is as wonderful as the heart. The heart just keeps on pumping, day and night and over the years, and the mind has its own way of keeping up with the world. For one thing, there's sleep. Thank God for it. When we sleep we get rest from all the pressure. And the dreams we have, even though we may forget them and wake up with the idea that we haven't dreamed, or even though they've been scary and have disturbed our sleep — well, those dreams are the mind's way of figuring out all that's bothering it. The series of pictures you call a dream is a story you tell to yourself and when it's done, things are in better control. All those different wishes and fears have been gathered up and made into something like a movie, you could say. It's better to have one part of your mind shaping itself up into a story and making sense to another part, than letting all the different things bothering us and tempting us go running around in their own little circles."

Cathy felt the doctor's eyes on her. She had lifted her head while listening to him but directed her eyes around the room. For a second their eyes met, but she quickly glanced downward. In her mind she was telling herself, I'm fine now. The doctor would never see her behave any other way. He really didn't know what it was like for her when she got one of those "attacks" or whatever they were. His reassurance was backfiring, making her feel misunderstood.

The doctor couldn't quite follow Cathy's line of thought but he sensed it. Cathy read it in his eyes and knew that he didn't know what to say. He was going to wait. They both suffered the awkwardness that dominated the room. Cathy felt uncomfortable; she *was* uncomfortable. After all, that was why she'd come to see him. At least he hadn't puffed her up with lectures, flattered her or bolstered her ego or patted her on the back expecting her to float out of his office and home.

"Well, Cathy," he ventured, "I'm sorry I can't wipe away your problems with a pill or a wave of my hand." He waved his hand then he sat there, silent.

Second after second ticked away and Cathy looked at her shoes and moved them in arcs, first one, then the other. Then, at last she spoke. "I'm sorry. I don't know what to say. I guess I'm just all mixed up. Do you think I'll ever get back to where I was? Should I take some medicine? I mean, not being able to sleep — that's serious — but I've never liked taking pills. Those headaches — even for them I hated to take aspirin. You don't think there's anything wrong with my head, do you? I thought to myself a few nights ago, while I was trying to do my homework, that maybe I have a brain tumor, something really bad like that. You get headaches then, don't you?"

He told her he could do some "brain-wave tests" but he was quite sure they'd be negative. She could take some medicine if she continued to have trouble sleeping but he doubted her insomnia would last. She might never again be the same person she was a couple of months ago, he told her. "It happens to all of us. We go through experiences and they may be demanding and exhausting, and we are to some extent changed by them. Often we are changed for the better, because we have been made to look more closely at ourselves, at our values and purposes, and in so doing we get more control over ourselves." He leaned forward in his chair and his eyes caught hers.

Cathy felt herself blush and looked away. He is so sure of himself, she thought. He talks like Mr. Aiken, our minister. They both have an answer for everything. Look at his forehead — not a line on it. He's probably never worried about anything in his whole life. He's always able to talk himself into being relaxed and cool.

Well, he's not talking me into anything. I feel as nervous as I did last night, when my mind was racing.

As all that went through her mind, she tried to avoid looking at the doctor, but he bore down on her with his eyes and would not let up with his optimistic predictions that soon, quite soon, she'd be much better. Finally, he said, "Next year this whole episode will seem part of the distant past," and she exploded. She leaped up from her chair and ran toward the door to his waiting room. She stopped just short of it, whirled around, glared at the doctor and felt a terrible impulse to pound on his desk. Instead, she screamed, "You don't know how I've been feeling. I'll be worse, much worse next year. I just know it. I wish you wouldn't keep saying all those nice things, telling me how wonderful everything is going to turn out to be. I really do wish you'd realize that I'm in danger of losing my mind. Worse than that, next year Rick will be gone and his parents will just love that, and then, *then* I won't care whether I have lost my mind or not." With that she started to cry, and as the doctor came toward her she let out more anger. "Please, don't try to tell me everything is going to be O.K. You've been doing that for hours, it seems like, and when I hear you say something I know isn't right, I get confused and it makes me think you really don't know what's going on."

There was no trace of a smile on his face as Dr. Strong answered her. "Cathy, it's not easy for one person to know another's mind. I'm no mind reader. Even the best psychiatrist in the world knows only as much as he's *told* by the patients who come to see him. A *bad* psychiatrist, as a matter of fact, is someone who jumps to conclusions about what his patients are thinking and going through without hearing the evidence from them. He reads *his* ideas and theories into *their* minds. So, I have to thank you, Cathy, for letting me know how *you* feel. Thanks for the warning you gave me. I probably *do* try to pat people on the back and say now, now, it's all going to be fine. I've seen so many young people come in here all worked up over something. They come sad and tense or afraid and then we've had a good talk. Maybe I've helped them with some medical problem — their skin is all broken out or their periods are irregular. They feel much better when they come back in a few weeks. But you've had a really rocky time and you don't want me just whistling along and serving you happy fortune cookies."

Cathy immediately took up where he had left off. "That's right. I didn't mean to be rude or mad, but I almost get lost sometimes. It's scary not knowing when you're going to feel half-paralyzed with all those crazy thoughts coming into your head. It's as if my head is sending sparks off in all directions. I sit there in my room and I would want to bury myself in the pillow and sleep, and at the same time I think back to when I was little and how nice it was just playing on the street with the other kids. Then I get those strange ideas about chewing up the thermometer, stupid ideas like that, and my head feels as though there's a huge oil well in it and the oil is pushing, pushing, but no one has figured out how to tap it and let it pour out, so I have to sit there and feel the pressure all over my head."

She stopped and came back toward the doctor. There were tears in her eyes and in her voice. There was more to come but she couldn't go on. The doctor sensed it, so he didn't say more than a yes. He gave her a concerned smile; he stood up and handed her a cup of water. Cathy took a sip, drew in a deep breath, and made a plunge. "Do you think . . . ?" She looked away.

He simply waited, but she felt the doctor's encouragement. His silence didn't make her nervous. In about half a minute she had composed in her mind what she wanted to say. "Doctor Strong, I've been wondering whether I ought to go see a psychiatrist about all this. Like you say, I don't think I'm crazy, but in the middle of those attacks, I think I come pretty near to being a little crazy, and I'm afraid they'll continue, the attacks, and I'll feel weaker and weaker. You get worn down after a while. So, I wanted to know . . ."

He sat back in his chair and said, "Yes." Then he hesitated and she felt grateful that he was honest enough to search his mind openly, right before her, and in silence.

"Cathy, I've been thinking," he said. "You've told me you want this thing taken very seriously, and I'm going to oblige. I know a woman, she's a psychiatrist and her special field is the problems of young people, like yourself. I'd like you to go speak with her a few times, if that's all right with you."

Cathy was stunned. She hadn't really expected to

be told she needed a psychiatrist. She felt she did, but she also felt it was a sign of how serious her troubles were — and so now she became even more worried about herself. Having unwittingly pushed the doctor to this, she resented it. She sat there trying to figure out whether she should go along with his advice, or should she ask to talk with him a few more times or even ask for the very thing she had shunned — some assurance that this was not a mental illness.

And what would her parents say? They would be shocked, she knew. They would interpret the recommendation as the worst possible news, and her father was still in debt from her grandfather's illness. Often he'd say he's working around the clock to "keep those doctors fat and happy." Now she would be adding that proverbial straw to his back. She sank lower and lower, so that in a few seconds she seemed glum indeed, as all those thoughts rushed through her mind, and grew into full-fledged scenes. She could picture her mother and father in the living room, telling her they'd find the money, and not for *her* to worry about things like that.

Had the doctor read her mind? Did he sense her

shock? His voice was low and very kind. "Cathy, can I suggest this? Would you be willing to come and see me a couple of times a week for the next few weeks? And next week, while we're going on with our talks, you could go and see Dr. Whitman, too. She's a friend of mine and I've talked with her from time to time about some of my patients and how I ought to work with them. She's sent patients to me because they've had some symptoms, some aches and pains, that she realizes need looking into. Now I *do* want to check out those headaches of yours even though I'd give you almost any odds you could dream of that you don't have anything pressing on your brain, a growth or something like that.

"How does that sound to you? I think it's important that we get talking with each other, and that you have a visit or two with Dr. Whitman. If she thinks it's necessary, a psychologist could do some tests that would tell us more about your mind and how it works. You know, everyone has his own way of thinking and settling problems. Once you've gone through all those visits, I think you'll get some understanding of what's happening to you and why it's happening now, at this particular moment in your life. Now you may say, what difference will that make, someone's explanation. You're here right now because you're *hurting,* that's the best word I know, but you don't really know why. Once you understand why, you can begin to control what's bothering you.

"Until I know which bacteria is causing an infection, I can't treat it. The same goes for the mind. We've learned in recent years that there's a cause-and-effect thing going on there, too. You don't just feel lousy for no reason at all. Something is scaring you or threatening you or making you feel overwhelmed, and the worst part about it is that often you don't know what that 'something' is." Cathy tried to interrupt. "I know, I know, you *do* have some hunches, and they're probably very good ones, but we're all our worst enemies. As I said before, the mind is a wonderful thing, it tries very hard to spare us pain, and in doing so it covers its tracks and we don't know a lot of what's ailing us because it's been pushed aside. When that strategy doesn't work we feel more and more at the edge of things. Our patience runs out and we're like jumping beans, nervously reacting to the slightest reminder of what's bothering us. And there you have it; the person is upset.

"But I'll tell you, Cathy, even the worst symptoms imaginable, even the worst you've been through, are not because your mind is 'cracking up,' or has thrown in the towel and given up trying to protect you. It's working hard to heal over the wounds you feel." Dr. Strong looked at his watch and smiled at Cathy. She still stood at the door but she felt quieter, somehow soothed. "Now we'll talk some more about this the day after tomorrow," he said, "It may just be that when you found yourself in that daze in the drugstore and afraid of the druggist's face, and later afraid of the man getting out of the Volkswagen — well, your mind was saying, I've got a lot bothering me. I'm not only growing up, I'm almost all grown up. I don't know what to do; I love Rick but that may not last because he's going away — in fact, he *is* away."

"And that's why I'm so sad I could just cry and cry? But I haven't cried and I can't. Maybe I'm worn down by all this, and maybe that druggist could have given me something for my nerves, except that if I had gone up and asked him, he'd have said no and been suspicious of me. And why when I look at people do they seem to be wondering about me, judging me?"

"Cathy, you are seeing your own fears in their faces. That's what we all do. When I feel good, I spot all the cheerful people around. I find plenty of confirmation for my high spirits. When I feel lousy, I notice the sour faces, and there are plenty of them. My wife jokes with me. She says that when I wake up in a good mood, I'll tell her that the birds are singing and it's a great world to be alive in. A week later I'll wake up early because I can't sleep, and something's worrying me, and I'll hear the birds going on and on, and I'll say that there must be a storm coming, because those birds sure do sound high-strung."

Cathy smiled. Even doctors can talk too much, she thought to herself. That crazy story about the birds; she knew what he meant. They could seem pretty nervous, chattering away, hundreds of them, as if there'd be rain any minute.

"Cathy," she heard. "I'm talking to you."

She jerked her attention back to Dr. Strong. She had been looking at him but not seeing. She dropped her gaze and said, "I'd like to go along with your plan. It sounds O.K. to me, and I just hope I'll get over this. The sooner the better."

"I hope so, too, Cathy."

On the way home Cathy felt better. At least she had shared her worries with someone, a doctor. She really wished that he had listened to her heart, had taken her blood pressure, looked into her eyes with that funny light, and come up with some medicine that would make her once and for all *cured*. She had pictured him calling in her parents the next day and telling them she needed an operation or some pills and other treatments, maybe X-ray. Now she sat in the car making conversation with her mother, telling her how much she liked Dr. Strong, what a good person he was, and how hopeful she was that everything would soon be "fine." But she kept wishing there *had* been a "disease or something," as she put it, that might have been immediately attacked with medicines or surgery. She even shared that wish with her mother, who told her to stop and think how awful surgery was.

And Cathy thought what an awful driver her mother

was, how hopeless her idea that psychological problems are better to have than those that can be cured with a few pills. So she fell silent and thought of Rick, then of Rick's father. She'd spoken to him when Rick was away, and had asked when Rick was due back. He'd teased her, told her "maybe never." "After all," he reminded her, "those college campuses are 'pretty attractive.'" She'd ignored that remark, among others. He had always been slightly fresh to her, much to Rick's displeasure. Rick didn't fight openly with his father, simply pulled further and further away from him. He was always apologizing for something his father had said to Cathy, though the two of them tried to stay away from the house, and keep friction down to a minimum. Cathy usually told Rick what his mother or father said to her. Often she just laughed it all off, knowing that her parents, when nervous, could also fumble with words and come up with jokes she politely called "very not funny." But that particular remark, about Rick maybe "never" coming back, had cut deep, so deep that she'd decided to keep it to herself. Besides, Rick might not come back. After all, Rick and she weren't engaged, nor had she ever believed they would be, however strongly he talked about their "future."

That talk with Dr. Strong had done nothing else, she thought to herself as they neared home, than remind her of that telephone conversation with Rick's father. For a minute or two she tried to place it. Did it happen at the beginning of Rick's trip, or later on, just before he came back? Well, it must have been toward the end — she certainly wouldn't have called at the beginning, when she knew he'd just left and would be away for some time. But why should that make her cross with Dr. Strong? And with her mother?

In spite of them, that night she slept like a log. She woke up glad to be going off to school, glad not to be waiting to see a doctor, glad that seeing him, then driving home and thinking about the visit was all behind her. She would be seeing Rick and that made her glad even though she'd be in that boring math class. Then it occurred to her that maybe she ought to be more worried than she was, maybe she was putting too much trust in the doctor. Maybe she was really freaking out.

As she approached school she found herself in a reverie — she was in a hospital, in a nurse's uniform, soothing a little girl's forehead with a cold cloth. She smiled to herself, then turned her attention to what was happening around her; one kid was pushing another and getting the same treatment back; a girl had just said good-bye to her mother, slammed the car door really hard and had started bad-mouthing both her parents to the friend who had ridden to school with her. A teacher was walking into the building, and some kids, including a friend of hers, were snickering behind his back. The bell rang, and everyone quickened his or her step.

She remembered her talk with Dr. Strong, and wondered why she was spotting all the unpleasant things. I feel in a better mood than I have in a long time, she insisted to herself, yet here I am chalking up every silly little sore spot that I can lay my eyes on. Then as she approached the door, she remembered that she'd always hated those few minutes before school. Once she'd told Rick that no one really wants to go to school, and that's why everyone is cranky and sullen before the first bell rings. They're just marking time before the show gets on the road, and taking it out on each other. Then she thought about that girl bad-mouthing her mother. She probably woke up feeling rotten and didn't even want to come to school, and her mother thought she'd do her a real big favor and bring her by car. It goes to show you, there's no point trying to be nice all the time, even to your own kids. Maybe if the mother had blown up, the girl would have blown up, too and maybe the kid would have been glad to be coming here, where at least she'd be with her friends.

The school door closed with a whoosh behind her and pictures flashed into her mind of fights with Rick, with her parents, one with her father and one with her mother, and then Francie, even with Dr. Strong. Suddenly it was funny and everything was in focus. Rick was *there*. She saw him coming down the hall and now she stopped all the thinking, the wondering and the figuring out. It would be enough to talk with him, to just be with him. Cathy grinned and almost ran toward him.

"Rick," she called. "Hi, Rick."

Pirates Can Work Together

Tom Easton

WINDMILL BOOKS

New York

Published in 2016 by **Windmill Books**,
an Imprint of Rosen Publishing
29 East 21st Street, New York, NY 10010

Commissioning editor: Victoria Brooker
Creative design: Basement68
Illustrations© Mike Gordon

Cataloging-in-Publication Data

Easton, Tom.
Pirates can work together / by Tom Easton.
p. cm. — (Pirate pals)
Includes index.
ISBN 978-1-5081-9159-9 (pbk.)
ISBN 978-1-5081-9160-5 (6-pack)
ISBN 978-1-5081-9164-3 (library binding)
1. Cooperativeness — Juvenile fiction. I. Easton,
Tom (Children's fiction writer). II. Title.
PZ7.E13159 Pir 2016
[F]—d23

Manufactured in the United States of America

CPSIA Compliance Information: Batch #BW16PK:
For Further Information contact Rosen Publishing,
New York, New York at 1-800-237-9932

Pirates Can Work Together

Written by
Tom Easton

Illustrated by
Mike Gordon

WINDMILL
BOOKS ™

New York

One hot day, on the *Golden Duck*,
Sam was hard at work in the galley,
making his speciality: Seven Seas Soup.

"The Captain likes a little salt in his soup," Sam
said to himself. "Though too much isn't good
for you." So he added a small pinch. As the soup
bubbled away, he went to help on deck.

"Get the mainsail down," the Captain shouted. "There's a storm coming."

Sam started winding the
capstan. It was
hard work.

"This is taking forever,"
the Captain said, as he watched
Sam sweat. "You need help."

The Captain went belowdecks to find someone
to help. As he passed the bubbling soup, he
stopped. "Sam never puts enough salt in," he
muttered, and added a pinch, but not too much!

Spying a foot poking out from behind
a barrel of pickled herring, the Captain went
to investigate. It was Davy, asleep as usual.
"WAKE UP!" the Captain roared.
"Sam needs help on deck."

Davy grumbled and slowly followed the
Captain. He did not want to help. He'd
been having a lovely dream about Davy's soup.

Licking his lips, he added a tiny pinch
of salt to the bubbling pot as he passed.
"Not too much," he thought to himself.

Sam hadn't gotten very far with the mainsail.
"Davy, you'd better start on the topsail,"
Captain Cod said, "or we'll be here all day."

Dark storm
clouds approached.

The two sails inched
down as the pirates heaved.

12

The Captain opened a hatch and shouted
for Pete to come and help.

"PETE!"

As Pete walked through the galley he added some salt to the soup for the Captain.

"One pinch is enough," he thought.

"Get that mizzen down,"
the Captain roared as Pete came up on deck.
"These two lubbers are taking forever.
We need to work on all three sails."

Sam sweated, Davy dripped, Pete perspired.
Even poor Polly Parrot tried to help by flapping
her wings to keep the captain cool. But still the
sails weren't coming down quickly enough.

"NELL," Captain Cod roared.

"NELL!"

17

The delicious smell of the soup had brought
Nell into the galley when she heard the Captain
call for her. There wasn't time to taste it, but
she knew Sam never put enough salt in
so she added a tiny pinch.

"These useless pirates have muscles
like noodles," the Captain fumed.
"Even working on all three sails at once,
it's going to take too long. The ship will
capsize and we'll all drown!"

"Wouldn't it be better if we all worked
together on each sail?" Nell suggested.
The Captain thought this over.

"What are you doing, you fools?" he yelled.

"You should all be working TOGETHER!"

"But..." Pete said.
"Don't argue,"
the Captain bellowed.
"Just do it!"
"We should help too,"
Nell said to the Captain.
"What? Oh, yes, I suppose so,"
the Captain said.

22

The pirates heaved and hoed.
Working together, the capstans turned much
more easily and the sails came down quickly.

"I knew my muscles would make the difference," the Captain said, looking around proudly once the work was done.

The pirates were exhausted after their efforts and had a little rest.

Polly went off to check on the soup. She knew the Captain liked a bit of salt and added the tiniest of pinches.

Suddenly the storm broke, sending all the pirates rushing belowdecks. As the ship rocked safely, they all sat down to dinner and the Captain gave a speech. "Thanks to my quick thinking..." the Captain began.

Nell coughed. "Thanks to Nell's quick thinking and my muscles," the Captain went on, "the ship was saved and we can all enjoy Davy's delicious soup. Perfect with just a little salt."

"Bleugh! Too much SALT!" the Captain shouted.

"That's strange," everyone said.
"I only added a pinch."

NOTES FOR PARENTS AND TEACHERS

Pirate Pals

The books in the *Pirate Pals* series are designed to help children recognize the virtues of good manners and behavior. Reading these books will show children that their actions have a real effect on people around them, helping them to recognize what is right and wrong, and to think about what to do when faced with difficult choices.

Pirates Can Work Together

Pirates Can Work Together is intended to be an engaging and enjoyable read for children aged 4-7. The book will help them to recognize why it's okay to ask for help and that working as a team can often bring better results.

When Captain Cod instructs the pirates to each work on a different sail, he is encouraging them to work separately, which makes the task harder. Nell realizes the Captain's mistake and communicates the solution. The Captain realizes the sense of her suggestion and orders the pirates to begin working as a team. The task is then completed quickly and easily.

Meanwhile, belowdecks, the pirates are, individually, adding salt to the soup, each believing they are working to the common good. Here, it's a lack of communication that leads to an unpleasant surprise for them all.

Being able to work together with others as part of a team is not just a skill needed at school or within a family, it is a vital skill used in all areas of life.

Teamwork requires people to work cooperatively with others to achieve a common goal. For a team to work together effectively, it is important for all members to respect each other's abilities and opinions. Teamwork is a social activity and involves interaction and exchanging of ideas. Being a team member will help children to communicate with others.

Working as part of a team will strengthen social and emotional skills, help develop communication skills, and can improve confidence.

At school, children will have to work in pairs, or in smaller or larger groups, depending on the task. They will work in teams for sporting activities. They will also tend to engage in unsupervised team activities at break times. Team activities can lead to competitiveness. Encourage children to be a good sport and a team player.

Suggested follow-up activities

Talk to the child about the events in the book. Why was it better that the pirates worked together in lowering the sails? How could the salty soup problem have been avoided?

Children can really enjoy being part of a team, but being excluded can be upsetting. Explain to them the importance of not excluding anyone and how upsetting it can be to be left out.

Ask them to work together on a team art project. Paint a mural as a group on a large sheet of paper or an old sheet.

Ask them to put on a short play, or hold an obstacle relay race. Ensure everyone has a clear role and a job to do.

BOOKS TO SHARE

I Can Make a Difference: A First Look at Setting a Good Example by Pat Thomas and Lesley Harker (Wayland, 2015)

This delightful picture book helps children to understand why it is important to have good manners and help others, and how consideration for others can make working and playing together more enjoyable for everyone.

Not Fair, Won't Share (Our Emotions) by Sue Graves (Watts, 2011)

Miss Clover has made a space station. Posy, Ben, and Alfie must take turns to play with it. But Posy doesn't want to share, and everyone gets mad. Can the children learn to work together and share?

Teamwork Isn't My Thing, and I Don't Like to Share by Julia Cook (Boys Town Press, 2012)

RJ has a bad day. He doesn't want to work in a group at school and has to share the last cookie with his sister. With help from his mom, he learns how working as a team and sharing can make him feel happy.